A Note to Parents and Caregivers:

Read-it! Readers are for children who are just starting on the amazing road to reading. These beautiful books support both the acquisition of reading skills and the love of books.

The PURPLE LEVEL presents basic topics and objects using high frequency words and simple language patterns.

The RED LEVEL presents familiar topics using common words and repeating sentence patterns.

The BLUE LEVEL presents new ideas using a larger vocabulary and varied sentence structure.

The YELLOW LEVEL presents more challenging ideas, a broad vocabulary, and wide variety in sentence structure.

The GREEN LEVEL presents more complex ideas, an extended vocabulary range, and expanded language structures.

The ORANGE LEVEL presents a wide range of ideas and concepts using challenging vocabulary and complex language structures.

When sharing a book with your child, read in short stretches, pausing often to talk about the pictures. Have your child turn the pages and point to the pictures and familiar words. And be sure to reread favorite stories or parts of stories.

There is no right or wrong way to share books with children. Find time to read with your child, and pass on the legacy of literacy.

Adria F. Klein, Ph.D.
Professor Emeritus
California State University
San Bernardino, California

Editor: Christianne Jones
Designer: Nathan Gassman
Page Production: Brandie Shoemaker
Creative Director: Keith Griffin
Editorial Director: Carol Jones
The illustrations in this book were created using graphite and digital mediums.

Picture Window Books
5115 Excelsior Boulevard
Suite 232
Minneapolis, MN 55416
877-845-8392
www.picturewindowbooks.com

Printed in the United States of America.

Library of Congress Cataloging-in-Publication Data
Blackaby, Susan.
Greg gets a hint / by Susan Blackaby ; illustrated by Zachary Trover.
p. cm. — (Read-it! readers)
Summary: Mom has a gift for Greg, but only after he guesses what it is from the strange
clues she gives him.
ISBN-13: 978-1-4048-2411-9 (hardcover)
ISBN-10: 1-4048-2411-1 (hardcover)
[1. Mothers and sons—Fiction. 2. Gifts—Fiction. 3. African Americans—Fiction.]
I. Trover, Zachary, ill. II. Title. III. Series.

PZ7.B5318Gr 2006
[E]—dc22   2006003572

Greg
Gets a Hint

by Susan Blackaby
illustrated by Zachary Trover

Special thanks to our advisers for their expertise:

Adria F. Klein, Ph.D.
Professor Emeritus, California State University
San Bernardino, California

Susan Kesselring, M.A.
Literacy Educator
Rosemount–Apple Valley–Eagan (Minnesota) School District

PICTURE WINDOW BOOKS
Minneapolis, Minnesota

"I have a surprise for you," Mom told Greg. "I'll give you a hint. It likes to play."

Mice like to play. Maybe it is a mouse, thought Greg.

"Will it fit in my hand?" asked Greg.

"No," said Mom. "It is bigger than your hand."

9

Cats are bigger than my hand. It might be a cat, thought Greg.

"Does it purr and meow?" asked Greg.

"No," said Mom. "It hoots and toots."

Owls hoot and toot. It might be an owl, thought Greg.

"Does it have a sharp beak?" asked Greg.

16

"No," said Mom. "But it comes with a trunk."

18

What likes to play, is bigger than Greg's hand, hoots and toots, and comes with a trunk?

Then Greg heard the doorbell.
"I know!" Greg yelled as he ran
to the door.

"Grandpa!" yelled Greg.
"What a great surprise!"

More *Read-it!* Readers

Bright pictures and fun stories help you practice your reading skills. Look for more books at your level.

Bears on Ice 1-4048-1577-5
The Bossy Rooster 1-4048-0051-4
The Camping Scare 1-4048-2405-7
Dust Bunnies 1-4048-1168-0
Emily's Pictures 1-4048-2409-X
Flying with Oliver 1-4048-1583-X
Frog Pajama Party 1-4048-1170-2
Galen's Camera 1-4048-1610-0
Jack's Party 1-4048-0060-3
Last in Line 1-4048-2415-4
The Lifeguard 1-4048-1584-8
Mike's Night-light 1-4048-1726-3
Nate the Dinosaur 1-4048-1728-X
One Up for Brad 1-4048-2418-9
The Playground Snake 1-4048-0556-7
Recycled! 1-4048-0068-9
Robin's New Glasses 1-4048-1587-2
The Sassy Monkey 1-4048-0058-1
The Treasure Map 1-4048-2416-2
Tuckerbean 1-4048-1591-0
What's Bugging Pamela? 1-4048-1189-3

Looking for a specific title or level? A complete list of *Read-it!* Readers is available on our Web site:
www.picturewindowbooks.com